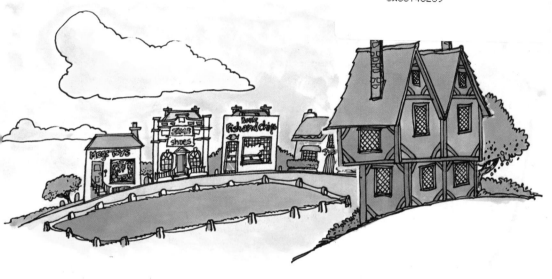

At the shops

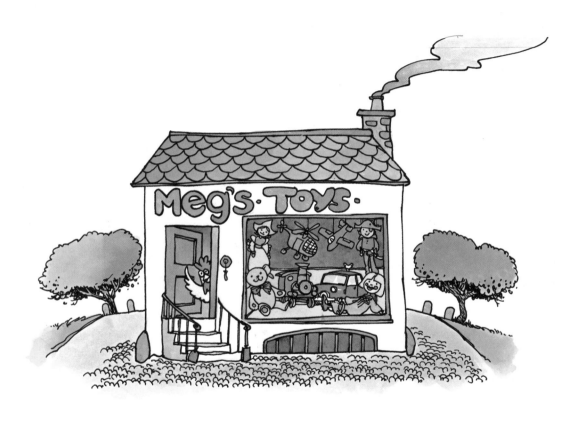

a toy shop

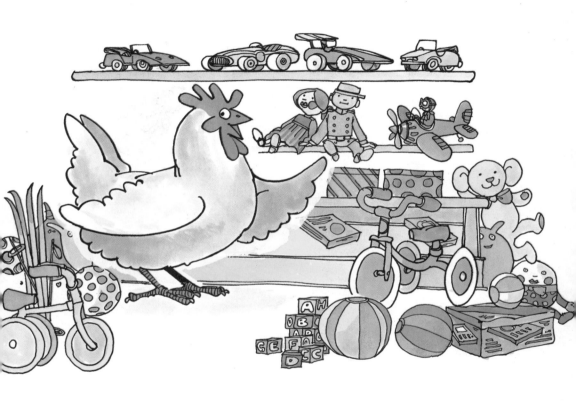

Meg the hen has a toy shop.

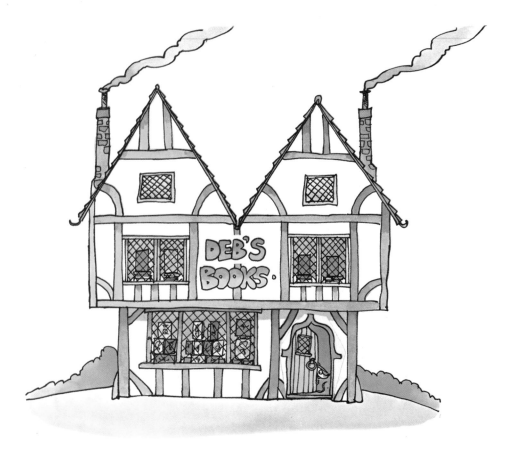

a book shop

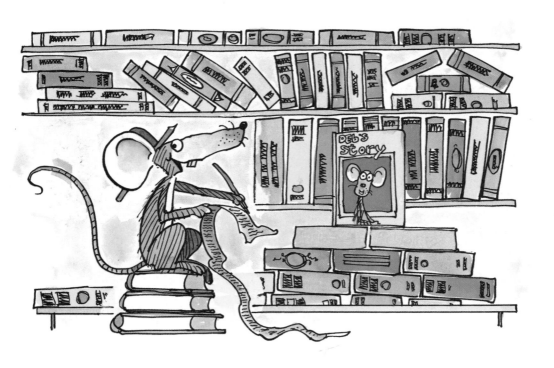

Deb the rat has a book shop.

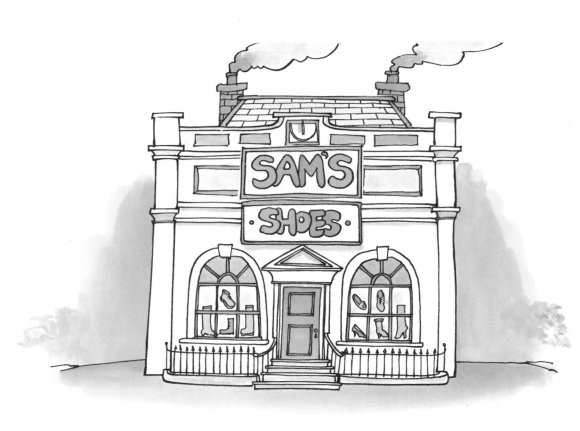

a shoe shop

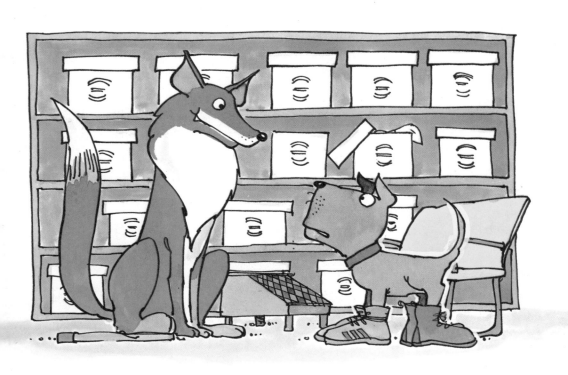

Sam the fox has a shoe shop.

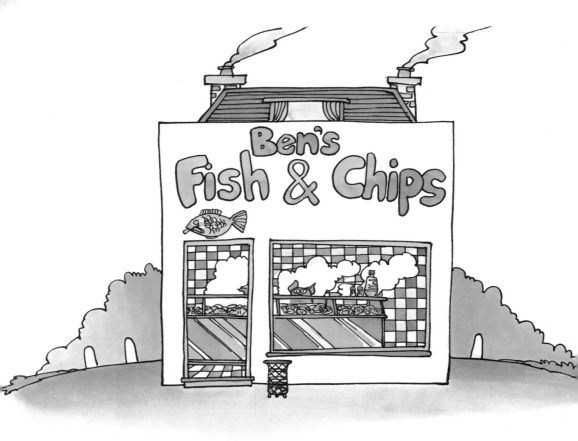

a fish and chip shop

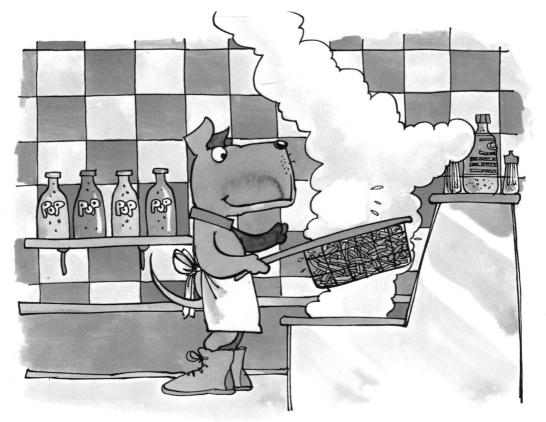

Ben the dog has
a fish and chip shop.

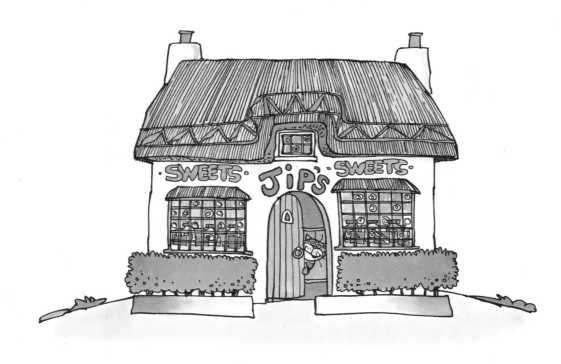

a sweet shop

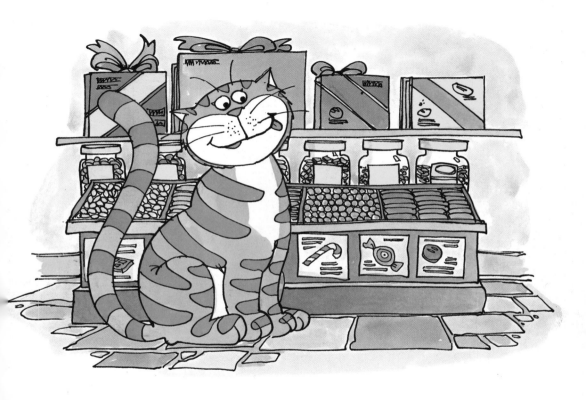

Jip the cat has a sweet shop.

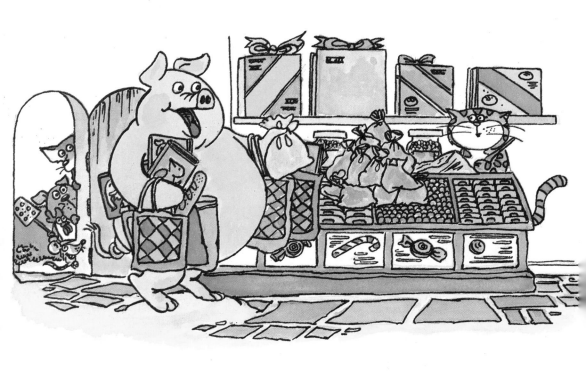

Fat Pig is at the shops.